My light among the waves

Justice Willoughby

CHAPTER 1

Arden

The engine of the rental car sighs as it stalls, almost relieved to rest after the more-than-three-hour drive since leaving Los Angeles. When I step out, the gravel in the Heisler Park car park crunches beneath my trainers, soaked in sand from other beaches, other memories. It's exactly the dawn I expected, with the horizon a bright orange hue and the Pacific gently churning as if still choosing the tone to start the day.

I stow my suitcase behind the seat and grab my SLR, my most trusted companion, a Nikon that still carries the smell of makeshift darkrooms and the red dust of Oaxaca. But I can't think about it now. Most of all, I don't want to. I push the thought of Evan away with all my might, as if it were an annoying detail I still have to erase from my life: I mustn't think about him, not now. I came to Laguna Beach to photograph the ArtWave for this reason alone. And it's an essential job for me right now, with good pay, room and board. An opportunity I couldn't pass up. Above all, it was the chance to get away from Los Angeles and him, enough to remind me who I was before I became a mere relic in his collection.

A particularly long wave crashes against the rocks, nearly splashing me with salty spray. I adjust the exposure, lower the aperture, and finally take the shot. In the viewfinder, the sun rises behind the wind-bent palm trees, and a pair of seagulls slices across the scene diagonally. With this evocative backdrop, I feel like a new phase in my life is beginning. I'm good at finding beauty in the cracks, and recently I've learned to actually do it; it's no longer just a slogan to post on social media for a few extra likes.

I shift my perspective when the sound of quick footsteps distracts me. A small, two-tone dog slips between my legs, wagging its tail eagerly. Behind it, a tall man approaches, even taller than me, athletic in build, dressed in a jogging suit that reveals his broad shoulders and sculpted calves. At first, I can only see his silhouette against the light, but my lens instinctively sharpens on him. He has short blond hair and a smile that captivates, wins, and seduces, even without intending to.

'Sorry, Jack is always far too lively early in the morning. I don't know how he manages it!'

His voice is cheerful yet deep, with a hint of a Midwestern accent that doesn't jar at all; rather, it creates a certain harmony within him. The dog—Jack, as I understand—barks as if confirming his owner's words.

'No problem,' I reply calmly, but my words are cut off as a wave, larger than expected, crashes over the stone wall and splashes straight towards us. Instinctively, I lift the SLR with both hands, but my soles slip on the wet moss. My heart jumps into my throat when I realise my camera is about to fall.

A strong arm snatches it from me just before it touches the water. The man, the blond one, spins around, using his chest as a shield. The SLR slams against his shirt and bounces off unharmed. I, on the other hand, lose my balance and end up sitting right on the wet ground.

'Nice dive off the ground!' His smile is genuine, incredibly warm and sunny. He extends his hand.

He has a broad, calloused palm, typical of someone who works with their body rather than just behind a computer. I let him pull me up, aware that my jeans are soaked and my face is flushed; I'm unsure whether it's from the cold water or embarrassment.

'Thank you, truly.' I embrace the SLR as if it were a child. 'I don't know what I would have done if…'

'Would you have cried for days?' The question acts as a provocation, with his grey-blue eyes glinting with bravado.

'Yes,' I admit, 'sort of.' My usually sharp sarcasm sounds dull this morning, almost shy.

He laughs heartily, a deep sound that unexpectedly delights me.

'Luke Whitaker,' he introduces himself. I sense that whatever he does in life, he does it with pride.

'Arden Morales.'

I shake his hand. His fingers are warm, despite the cool breeze. The contact lasts perhaps a second longer than necessary, long enough for my stomach to twist pleasantly; a gentle alarm, but an alarm nonetheless.

Jack barks again before sniffing the padded case I carry over my shoulder. He seems to approve, in his own way.

'Are you here to take photos of the festival?' Luke asks, switching the leash from one hand to the other. I see the sincere curiosity lighting up his face, as if he feels obliged to get to know every person he meets on the shore.

'Yeah. I have a contract to document ArtWave for the final catalogue.'

I try to sound casual, but I know I'm subtly bragging about the opportunity I've been offered, an old reflex that's stayed with me ever since I felt I always had to prove myself.

'So, in a way, we're colleagues.' He shakes his head and runs his fingers through his slightly messy hair. 'I run a boutique hotel nearby: the High Tide. During the festival, we host some artists and serve as a venue for performances. You know, sea, sunset, excellent wine, good food... stuff that's making Instagram go wild.'

That's why he seemed so at ease on this beach: he's the host.

'Interesting,' I reply, trying not to stare at his arms and muscular chest. Honestly, I don't. Or at least I try.

'Listen…' he continues, and I have no idea what he's about to say. 'Well, I was thinking... for saving you that expensive thing, I think it's fair to invite you to dinner in return. It's on me, and you'll be my guest, of course. I have an in-house restaurant that makes smoked oysters worthy of a physical and spiritual rebirth.' He raises an eyebrow and gives me a look, halfway between a challenge and a romantic invitation.

9

His request hits me like a cold wave. Instinctively, I take a step back. Dinner with him means stepping out of my professional comfort zone, sharing my thoughts, perhaps even laughing with someone I don't know well enough, and risking being hurt and, even worse, getting involved. After Evan, after his ability to turn every confidence into a weapon against me, I'm no longer sure I know how to judge boundaries. I'm still too vulnerable, that's for sure.

'I appreciate the invitation,' I whisper, struggling to find the strength to decline and resist the temptation. Luke Whitaker is a damned attractive man. 'But I still have to unload all the gear, settle into the hotel... And then I must prepare the schedule for tomorrow's shoot. Maybe another time.'

I notice my voice stiffen, even as I try to soften it with a half-smile. It's difficult to refuse, but I have no choice. And then... well, maybe his only intention is simply to be kind, not necessarily because he has an ulterior motive.

Luke nods, but I notice a flicker of disappointment behind his friendly facade.

I understand. The offer is still available, though. The High Tide is on Cliff Drive, two blocks to the north. Feel free to stop by anytime, even if it's just for a coffee. Jack will appreciate some company.

'Thanks, I'll keep that in mind.'

The dog wags its tail. I clear my throat and point the camera towards the sea to signal that the conversation is over, at least for now. Luke whistles a call, and Jack bounds onto the path, his tail wagging happily. Then he turns one last time, raising his hand in greeting. The sun, finally above the horizon, almost seems to draw a golden halo behind his hair.

I take a deep breath. The salt stings my dry lips, and my heart races a little too fast. Inside me, I feel like two voices are constantly at odds: one desperately wants to accept that invitation, while the other reminds me of the pain I still carry on the walls of my soul, invisible on the outside but constantly throbbing.

I look around for a few more moments before getting into the car. On the map they sent me, I see that the festival organisers have booked me a hotel nearby, marked only as "HT – Suite 3". I glance at the abbreviation, and it takes me a moment to connect the dots. Even the street matches.

HT. High Tide? It can't be, damn it!

'No...' I mutter to myself, turning the key in the ignition. The engine starts, the radio tunes to a local station playing an '80s ballad that's decidedly too sentimental for my tastes. I pull out of the parking lot as the light grows stronger over the bay.

If the festival booked me a room at Luke's hotel, then that missed dinner isn't a final goodbye but rather an inevitable "see you later." And I'm not ready at all. I check my email again: the reservation is already paid, non-refundable. A whole month, damn it, to document everything! Fate isn't on my side.

A whole month with the man with grey-blue eyes who seemed to almost read me without even realising it. A whole month trying to hide and keep away from an inevitable attraction towards him.

I close the email and sigh, feeling resigned. The steering wheel slips beneath my slightly sweaty fingers. At this stage of my business trip, there are no emergency exits that won't send me plunging back into the void I escaped from.

Meanwhile, the Pacific Ocean continues crashing beside the road I am travelling along. I wonder if I will be able to keep pace or if I will end up submerged again.

In any case, I've already taken the coastal route. I can't go back, nor even change my destination. I must accept the challenge; there's no turning back that can truly alter the course set by this new wave of destiny.

CHAPTER 2

Luke

The inviting aroma of roasted coffee drifts around, blending with the subtler, almost hidden scent of beeswax freshly applied to the teak handrail. This is exactly the fragrance I want to greet my guests with as they cross the threshold of High Tide. A promise of warmth after the Pacific breeze, like a gentle touch that says, "You can relax here; you're safe.'

It's a pity I'm the only one who never quite manages to do so. I'm too absorbed in the various problems and dilemmas, real or imagined, that constantly build up, making my life a constant struggle.

Anyway, it's best not to dwell on me and my almost non-existent private life. Better to focus on work, which, after all, is the only thing that gives me genuine satisfaction.

'Raphael, ensure the sheets for Suite 3 are raw linen, not Egyptian cotton. The artist arriving today prefers breathable fabrics, as mentioned in the booking email we received.'

My concierge nods patiently, like someone who understands I scrutinise every detail not out of delusions of grandeur but out of necessity. The truth is, after thirty-two years of life, I've become a perfectionist—perhaps even a little pedantic—to satisfy another voice that has always been loud inside me: Jocelyn Whitaker, my mother, the queen of etiquette in Cedar Falls, Wisconsin. My recurring nightmare now is that, in a few days, unless she changes her mind before leaving, she'll be in the lobby, inspecting everything with the same severity she once ran her finger across our kitchen countertop, searching for any hidden specks of dust that hadn't been properly swept away.

I try to relax with a deep breath. The sea beyond the windows is lit up by the afternoon light. ArtWave officially starts tomorrow, but most of the artists have already arrived in irregular waves. The hotel has become a store of easels, cello cases, and boxes of coloured LEDs. I've printed out a programme with codes for the rehearsal rooms, taped maps in the hallways, and set out bowls for my dog Jack (a real sly dog when it comes to disappearing food) to stop him from sneaking croissants. But I still feel immersed in that typical chaos my mother would call "unprofessional", with her cold, detached tone that always turns a compliment into a rebuke.

Sarah Lloyd, one of ArtWave's lead curators, greets me at reception. Her black helmet gleams under the rattan lamp.

'Good morning, Luke. Tonight, we're setting up the platform on the observation deck for Mars's performance. Can I borrow your 220V outlet?'

'Borrow anything you want, Sarah, except my patience,' I joke and wink. 'I'm afraid I have very little left.'

'Don't worry, boss,' Sarah laughs. 'If you like, I'll swap you my constant races against time! But I'm still sure we'll succeed... and that it will be a great triumph!'

I envy her confidence; despite everything, Sarah remains convinced she is in the right place, as if she has always known it. I, on the other hand... I just don't know anything sometimes. It's as if my certainties are in a constant struggle to persuade me to move forward, to make progress in the attempt to achieve something good, for myself and others.

Anyway, I seize the opportunity to take another tour of the rooms still waiting to welcome new guests, checking that everything is in perfect order.

The globe lamps cast an amber light on the sand-coloured walls, the diffusers waft bergamot notes.

Suite 3, the one reserved for Arden Morales, is ready to welcome him: linen bedding, a welcome basket of figs and pistachios, a handwritten note (*"If you need anything, call 101, Luke"*). In the end, I admit that the tour of the rooms was an excuse. This is exactly where I wanted to be. To wait for him. To see that intense gaze again, that golden skin, those amber eyes.

I shake my head, feeling like an idiot. I shouldn't even be thinking about it after he turned down my dinner invitation. Even then, I was "unprofessional", to be honest. I should have held back, but I couldn't resist.

I leave my key ring on the coffee table, determined to depart. But instead, I turn to look around the room, retrace my steps, approach the bed, and gently smooth out a non-existent crease on the pillow.

As I leave, the silence of the hallway envelops me and reminds me that I may never truly be able to overcome my own perfectionism. But, what's even worse, I won't be able to overcome my instincts, which always lead me down impassable paths, unattainable hopes, and dreams that will probably never come true. And it's precisely to this that I will have to surrender, sooner or later. Unrealised dreams: my torment, my condemnation.

CHAPTER 3

Luke

It's nearly midnight when I flop onto the sofa in my ground-floor apartment. Jack is curled up asleep, his face resting on the pillow he's claimed as his territory. On the coffee table, I hear a notification ring: an email from my mother. I read the same sentence three times. She plans to arrive even earlier than expected. So, she has no intention of changing her mind. Fine, that means I'll have to deal with it.

The intercostal muscle beneath my right shoulder blade tightens, as if to warn me that my margin for error is narrowing. I still need to muster the courage to tell her that her good and devoted son won't give her a blond, dimpled grandson, but he has already given his heart to a man once and might do so again. It wasn't merely a desire to experience something new and different. It wasn't simply a phase, above all.

An impulse urges me to head out; I need some fresh air. I slip on my flip-flops and sweatshirt. Jack, hearing the creak of the door, tilts an ear and gives me a sceptical look. I step back and pat his head.

'You stay here and keep watch, General.'

He narrows his eyes and yawns, his mouth wide open. I interpret this as a "go ahead." It's clear to me that he's not even considering coming out with me to keep me company.

The night on the beach appears like velvety blue, highlighted by the glow of houses perched on the cliffs. The surf sounds like a hypnotic mantra, helping me breathe deeply. There, between the black line of the water and the now greyish edge of the sand, I see a figure bent over a tripod. An SLR aimed at the night sea, his shoulders wrapped in a flannel shirt unbuttoned at the sleeves, despite the night breeze.

During the day, amidst one errand and another, I missed his arrival at the High Tide.

But it's him. Undoubtedly him. Arden.

I slow my pace to avoid disturbing him. However, the flash doesn't fire. He's simply using a long exposure, allowing the phosphorescence of the plankton to light up the scene. Suddenly, I understand; he's trying to capture bioluminescence, that electric blue that flickers in seconds. It's a phenomenon that requires infinite patience, a little trust, and a great deal of love for his craft. From his intense gaze, I can tell this is exactly how he feels. He loves his work, and it shows.

I take a few steps closer but maintain a safe distance. I see his face in profile, marked by a couple of days' worth of unkempt beard. His amber eyes narrow to focus, a stray lock of hair falls onto his forehead, and he pushes it away almost angrily, too absorbed to care. He hasn't noticed me, so I can observe him calmly.

I notice that his movements are slow and deliberate, as if he is asking the sea's permission before stealing a secret. At this moment, he appears more vulnerable than ever, and I find myself folding my arms across my chest, as if I could hold all that unexpected beauty in a hug.

I hear a click. Arden lowers the camera and checks the shot on the screen. That's when he lifts his rolled-up sleeve a few inches, moving his arm to reveal a thin but rather long, slanting scar just inside his left wrist.

I take another step forward, but as if I've stepped on an invisible wire, fear still holds me back. Meanwhile, I begin to reflect and process. Perhaps I'm exaggerating my assumptions; a scar can have multiple meanings. Sometimes it's a cry for help, other times a warning not to ask uncomfortable questions. I remain suspended between two opposing instincts: the desire to take his hand and ask him to tell me, to share parts of himself I'd like to know, and the fear of setting off an alarm that would close all doors before I even try to knock.

The sand crinkles softly beneath my feet. Arden, as if drawn by an unseen call, suddenly turns towards me. His eyes widen, then soften as he recognises me.

'Couldn't you sleep either?' he whispers, as if the night compels him to lower his voice. He doesn't mention that he has arrived here, as if he assumes we both expected to meet again.

'The sea sometimes has that effect.' I don't know what else to say, and he constrains himself to a crooked smile. 'It has its secrets.'

'I think I borrowed one.' He lifts his SLR camera and leans closer to show me the display. The sea looks like a carpet of stardust, the waves are outlined in transparent profiles, and Arden's figure stands at the left edge of the frame, like a dark silhouette between two worlds of light.

'If you can print that photo large enough, I'd like it in my foyer' I ask him with a sincerity that frightens me. 'I'm willing to pay, of course.'

His smile cracks, perhaps from embarrassment.

'We'll see.'

He lowers his gaze, and I notice him folding his right forearm over his left, hiding the scar in a gesture that seems too instinctive to be deliberate. Perhaps it's just a habit.

I realise it's time to ask, now or never. But it's as if my tongue is stuck to the roof of my mouth. Or maybe it's my mother's imminent arrival that's holding me back.

In any case, I summon my courage and try to be as natural as possible.

'Tomorrow at seven, Jack and I will go for our usual walk. If you need a model, you're welcome to come along. By model, I mean Jack...'

I'm not sure how the request was made, but I still feel like an idiot.

Arden chuckles softly.

'Leave your poor dog be. But thanks, anyway.'

I nod and smile. We stand for a few seconds, gazing out at the sea in silence. It might feel like an awkward silence, but as the minutes pass, it becomes almost comforting. We're little more than strangers, I know, but it's as if we've found a common ground. Or, perhaps, even more than one.

As we walk towards the hotel, our shadows pass close without touching. I wish they could, but I don't hurry and I don't try to get any closer than necessary. He holds the SLR with both hands, his thumbs tapping on the camera, perhaps his mind is already processing the image, adjusting the curves, calibrating the contrasts.

The entrance to the High Tide is lit by LED lanterns. The revolving door shows our reflections. I smile at the thought of what might happen if we loosen up, but I try not to cross any lines.

'I'd like to take this opportunity to offer you my personal welcome to High Tide.' I smile at him, trying to seem as relaxed and confident as possible. 'Goodnight, Arden.'

'Thank you. Goodnight, Luke.'

We each head off in our own direction from the hallway. But there's a moment, perhaps only imagined in my mind, when I feel us both turn at the same time. Yet we're already too far apart for any real confirmation.

I reach my room and lie down on the bed, kicking off my shoes. A few minutes later, my phone vibrates on the bedside table. I check the message, and the name "Mom" appears. I swallow before scrolling through the preview.

"Did you receive my email? I'm arriving earlier than expected, love. I can't wait to see your wonderful hotel all prepared for the big event!"

That exclamation mark is more forceful than all the other words combined. Earlier than expected. I bite my lip and sigh. The truth is that "earlier than expected" unsettles me, almost like a threat. I can't help but wonder: why now? Above all, I can't help but blame fate and, to some extent, myself for never having been able to speak clearly to her. Not really, at least.

I feel a throbbing sensation in my head and a heaviness in my chest at the same time. I scroll through other conversations, then go further up, pausing on an old message where I confessed, in just a few words, that I was attracted to a man. Shortly after, I also mentioned that I was having an affair with a man. Her response was nonchalant, as if it were just a phase I would soon get over.

"Surely it is only a temporary moment."

But no. It's not like that. She'll be here soon, and I fear I'm not ready to face it, nor am I ready to pretend that everything is surmountable. Especially not this time. What constitutes a "temporary moment" for her is my daily reality, my life.

I close my eyes, but the image of Arden, vulnerable and beautiful, taking photographs of the sea at night, reappears before me like a protective shield. I'd like to borrow his ability to look into chaos and see the light, to grasp it, to take it out. Or perhaps I'd like him to be my light. My light among the waves.

Instead, I remain still, like a ship's captain who fears the storm before setting sail, worried about being completely submerged.

Soon, I'll need to gather the courage to reveal myself once and for all and face the consequences. I can no longer hide or try to make the truth seem less shocking. This is who I am, and I finally want to be accepted and understood exactly as I am.

CHAPTER 4

Arden

I understand it as soon as I step onto the beach. The ocean today isn't just a backdrop; it's the real star. The mid-morning sun reflects off everything—the beach, the sea, and the surfboards that bravely cut through it. At the centre of it all are Sarah Lloyd, the brilliant curator of ArtWave, and Marcus Delgado, also known as Mars, an artist always ready to turn his emotions into poetry. They seem perfectly at ease. I've known them for some time, and I enjoy working with them.

Sarah, always a steadfast optimist in everything she attempts, wears a light black wetsuit adorned with a few small tattoos: stylised waves extending from her wrist to her elbow and curious geographic coordinates engraved along her neck. She moves her hands decisively, instructing some participants on posture and stroke style. Mars, in contrast, wears a glittery lavender wetsuit and a fluorescent fuchsia helmet that defies conventional taste. Occasionally, he blows a golden whistle and recites some impromptu verse.

I clutch the SLR and sigh, half-deceiving myself into thinking that I'm not being noticed and that I'm staying safe behind the lens. Just then, Sarah gives me a searching look, penetrating yet benevolent.

'No comfort zone for you today, Morales! You won't hide behind the lens!'

I smile, nod, and roll my eyes. Then I give a confident thumb-up; I know I won't win against Sarah, she's so stubborn. But meanwhile, my heart beats that wrong note that resonates inside me every time I risk trying to truly live. To truly feel something.

At that precise moment, I see Luke running across the beach with Jack circling him. He's wearing a short wetsuit that contours his broad shoulders and muscular thighs, reminiscent of a former swimmer. His blond hair, still dry, falls partly over his eyes until he shakes it away with a gesture that's probably involuntary but sensual, to the point that he looks like a commercial model. I almost instinctively take in the scene: him laughing with amusement, his surfboard under his arm, Jack bouncing around him, and the Pacific forming a bluish arena behind them.

I take the shot. Once, then again, and again, I feel like I can never get enough. In a split second, I've captured something that even my conscience hadn't noticed. Luke suddenly turns and looks at me with an expression that mixes adrenaline and surprise, as if he realises, at that very moment, that I'm simultaneously disorienting and comforting him.

Then he moves confidently towards me.

'Did you catch me when I wasn't posing?' he smiles, moving closer. 'It's not fair playing jokes like that!'

His deep voice vibrates and echoes in my chest. I can almost feel it inside me, almost physically. So I raise my SLR, like a shield, as if to defend myself from him and, above all, from my own feelings.

'I only give people what they deserve,' I retort, but the joke sounds less sharp and biting than I intend. I try to make amends. 'And I capture them at their best, if I can. If they let me.'

'Perfect.' He swivels the board under his arm, then unexpectedly, he extends his free hand towards me. 'Now it's your turn to earn your lunch and also pay me back for those stolen photos. Come in the water with me.'

Damn, I've gotten myself into trouble unintentionally!

I'm searching for an excuse, any excuse—more than one. Sarah needs me to provide some high-resolution images; I also have to prepare more shots for the ArtWave project... I just don't know what else to come up with!

But Luke doesn't give me any more time. 'Your work certainly won't suffer if you indulge in some fun.'

So, he grabs the strap of my SLR, unclips it from my shoulder, and passes it to Mars, who cheers.

'Don't worry, Arden. I'll safeguard your treasure! You go and enjoy yourself, you deserve it!'

'I'm no good at surfing,' I protest, turning to Luke. 'I've never actually learned, that's all! I'm a disaster.'

'Great. I'll teach you. I am a good instructor.'

His grey-blue eyes shine with a closeness that leaves me breathless. This isn't right. This isn't right at all.

Instead, despite myself, I find my feet on the board, trying to keep my balance. The water bites my calves with the first undertow and rises towards my thighs. It's cold, alive. Luke is right in front of me, his knees bent and his hands open. He explains how to balance my weight, how to control my body, where to keep my gaze. He speaks slowly, confidently, making every instruction he gives me seem like an ancient, essential secret. When the first wave lifts us, I cling to his forearm as if it were the mast of a ship in a storm. He laughs, his low, infectious laugh, which overwhelms me even more than the Pacific waves.

The wave, merciless, knocks us both into the water. I feel as if I'm drinking in the entire Pacific; I surface coughing but laughing at the same time. Luke helps me back up, urging me to try again. After three attempts, I finally manage to stand, even if only for a few seconds, long enough for the cool, light breeze to stir a feeling of pure joy inside me. I mentally snap a photo — a picture of us, still unsteadily balanced, but with the luminous sea surrounding us, holding us together, bonded.

When we emerge from yet another attempt, I see Mars aiming his camera at us, ready to take the shot. I can picture my expression in the photograph he's just snapped, next to Luke. At that moment, for the first time in too long, I realise I'm not afraid of being seen, of being accepted. Above all, I'm not afraid of what I'm starting to feel.

CHAPTER 5

Arden

Around one o'clock, Sarah announces the class is over, and everyone heads to the kiosk on the pier. I dry myself with a coarse towel, feeling my skin nearly burn from salt and sun. I almost experience the sensation of feeling more alive than ever.

Luke and I also head towards the kiosk, which appears to be in perfect California style: psychedelic murals, succulent snacks for all tastes, the aroma of fried tortillas. We order two plates of birria tacos and sit on one of the wooden benches arranged around it. Luke takes a hearty bite of his taco, with the fervour of someone who hasn't eaten in days. Then he looks up and stares at me.

'So, what do you think of California, the ocean, and especially surfing?'

'I've been in California for a while, but here I find everything incredible—somewhat frightening yet strangely welcoming and familiar at the same time. But I don't think what I'm saying makes any sense.'

I'm beginning to lose my grip on my words and expressions, I'm worried. Was I really talking about California and surfing... or about him? I bite into my taco in an effort to look away and hide my feelings.

'It does make sense, though. I believe I understand what you mean.'

He bursts into laughter. And I laugh because he does, and I can't help myself. The sound blends with the music from the kiosk, the cries of the seagulls, the laughter of others and of Mars and Sarah, who are arguing about the level of spiciness of the salsa, too much for him and not enough for her.

Luke passes me a paper napkin and, as he does, brushes his fingers over my hand. It's a minimal touch, but it feels scorchingly hot, at least to me. To distract myself from the contact, I try to say something—the first thing that comes to mind.

'I always try to find a little light in the cracks. It's my recurring theme, I believe, even in the images I attempt to capture.'

'Light in the cracks...' he repeats, as if savouring the words, in his deep, almost hoarse voice. 'I think I understand, but could you explain it better?'

I nod and take a deep breath. The thought of Evan, of his abuse of me, surfaces, but I try to push it away, to erase it. I don't want to let the flow drag me into the abyss, risking never being able to surface again.

'It's about...' I bite my lip for a moment, then force myself to swallow. I don't want to make a mistake in what I'm trying to express. I also don't want Luke to misunderstand or judge me unfairly. 'It's about finding glimmers of light where no one looks any more, where no one searches for them. Broken people inside, abandoned houses, forgotten objects. Photographing them is how I remind myself that even in something broken, there can be so much beauty...'

Luke tilts his head. His eyes glaze over briefly, but maybe it's just the reflection of the sun. Or perhaps it's only my imagination.

'And when you can't find that light?' he asks. 'What do you do?'

'I make it up.' I smile, but the smile fades halfway, betrayed by a distant ache, like a discomfort rising from beneath my sternum and spreading inside me. 'Or at least I try.'

Luke nods slowly. He bites off the last piece of taco, then flicks the paper into the bin with sporting elegance.

'I believe you're much braver than you realise, Arden.'

The unexpected compliment surprises me. I'm about to reply, but I feel a vibration from my phone inside my backpack.

I check my phone and see an Instagram notification: @evanclarke_therealvision liked my stories this morning, three times, 20 seconds ago. In those three stories, besides other people at ArtWave, Luke was also clearly visible. More than the others, damn it!

My blood runs cold in my veins despite the sun warming my skin and body. I put my phone back in my backpack, trying, perhaps in vain, to keep control. Luke, however, doesn't take his eyes off me; he's far too attentive to my movements and body language.

'Everything okay?' He frowns.

I nod too quickly.

'Yes, of course. Nothing much, just work.'

'The photography world must be very competitive, I imagine.' Maybe he believes me, but I fear he's caught the shadow that just crossed my face. However, he thinks it's work, so much the better.

I force myself to smile and shrug, but I can't relax or let go like I used to.

The rest of the time, I try to really focus on work, to let the oppressive thoughts of my relationship with Evan Clarke fade away.

In the late afternoon, the impromptu photo editing session on the ground floor of the High Tide completely distracts me. As hours pass, I relive the shots and moments I captured: Sarah lifting the board above her head, Mars laughing with water droplets suspended like glitter, Luke grabbing my waist as the wave engulfs us. Each image is a treasured moment, a flash of light that finally brings me back to the surface after surviving the abyss, the darkness. Hell.

But the echo of that damned Instagram notification disrupts the harmony I've painstakingly built. Evan looked. Evan saw. Which means Evan knows. Evan has certainly noticed Luke in my stories. He's always been very aware of my gestures, my glances, and the other men around me.

I try to reassure myself that posting a happy moment isn't a crime, and that I have every right to a present and a future. But when I take the lift to Suite 3, a feeling of unease and fear grips the pit of my stomach, unable to be quelled.

I open the door and look around. The room appears the same as this morning, apart from one detail: on the bed, perfectly centred beneath the sand-coloured bedspread, there's a medium-sized printed photograph. As I move closer, I notice that the image is neatly torn in half.

I recognise it instantly. It's me and Evan, about a year ago, posing in front of a mural in Los Angeles. I've got the lens in my hand; he's got his arm on my shoulder and is giving me a flirtatious look.

A hiss escapes my throat, almost a gasp. There are no tickets, nothing else. Just that image, along with the likes on my three stories. Like a silent warning: *"I see you. I'm always here. I won't let you go."*

I shift my gaze towards the door of the room I left half-open, as if expecting him to appear, grab me again, and finally destroy me. But the hallway is empty, quiet, almost too silent.

'*Maldito…*' the word slips out in Spanish, the familiar language I often speak at home when I visit my parents. The language I use to soothe myself, when I want to exorcise my demons. And Evan is my demon par excellence.

He's somewhere nearby. He found me and got to me. As usual, after all.

I go to close the door, turn the key, lean my back against the wood, and place a hand on my chest, trying to calm myself and my breathing.

The late afternoon sun filters through the curtains, casting golden streaks on the torn photograph.

'Light in the cracks' I repeat to myself. Light in the cracks. But this crack is too deep; no amount of light can heal it.

I clench my fists until I can feel nails digging into my flesh. I need to decide what to do. Should I tell Luke? Should I share my situation with him? But why should I? What could it possibly matter to him?

What options do I have? Stay silent and pretend nothing happened? Because telling Luke what occurred here, about the intrusion I experienced in my room at the High Tide, would mean... revealing everything. About my past, my private life.

At the same time, I realise that, as the person in charge, he should be aware, but…

Suddenly, a laugh from outside, perhaps from Sarah or another girl, reaches me, light and calm. Outside, life continues to flow peacefully. Inside, however, I feel the old abyss opening up beneath me again, ready to swallow every single glimmer of light from a day when I had managed to savour something like happiness, the desire to open my heart to someone again.

CHAPTER 6

Luke

If there's one thing I've learnt in my experience as a hotelier, it's that hospitality can make even the darkest sky shine. Tonight, the lobby at the High Tide appears brighter than ever, with its pendant lamps and soy candles flickering on the elegantly decorated tables. But the true beauty and touch of class that make the lobby unparalleled are the soft projections of Arden's photographs on the sand-coloured walls. Every three seconds, the Pacific Ocean emerges from one of the displays and transforms into waves of light and a stroke of liquid ink behind her signature: *Arden Morales - Light in the Cracks*.

Jack sleeps peacefully behind the bar, exhausted from the rush and the numerous compliments he has received throughout the day. Raphael and the other staff pass around flutes of Californian champagne, and Sarah, dressed in a black, off-the-shoulder gown and wearing a headset, carefully manages the flow of guests. I simply stand in the background, my heart pounding slightly as I try to follow Arden as he gazes at the panels with his larger prints.

Now, as the clear evening ascends from the sea and the first round of applause fades into enthusiastic words and chatter, I continue to search for him. I finally spot him next to the central panel, the one with the surreal bioluminescent sea, his outline barely visible at the edge. He's wearing a light jacket, his brown hair still slightly damp and tousled, his amber eyes seemingly conveying much more than words could. He's conversing with Mars, seemingly engrossed in a discussion about the images on display.

I walk towards them, convincing myself that now is the perfect time to try to figure out where to take our "relationship", if you could call it that—the undeniable electricity that has developed between us since our first encounter. And it seems to be growing in intensity at a relentless pace over the few hours we've spent together. I must understand; the moment has come. To know if Arden feels the same or if it's just my idea, my hunch.

So, I walk the short distance that separates us. Four steps, three, two... And only then do I see him. A tall man, with a lean yet muscular build beneath a midnight blue suit so flawless it appears tailor-made for him. His dark hair is slicked back, his jawline well-defined, a smile as measured as if it were a commercial.

I don't need the identification card, which Arden, after all, never bothered to show me. I can tell it's him — the guy who's been liking Arden's Instagram photos quite a lot, especially those from the past few months. I feel like a miserable stalker, but I checked his profile and found out that the man is none other than Evan Clarke, Arden's ex (maybe not so ex anymore).

In any case, as far as I'm concerned, Evan Clarke entered this evening like a knife mercilessly sliding down my back, carving a furrow inside me and planting itself between my shoulder blades. Meanwhile, I notice Arden's spine stiffen for a moment before he decides to move or at least attempt to. Then I see him move forward, as if the room suddenly tilted and someone forced him to slide towards that sneaky, insidious-looking person. But it's very likely that my judgment of him is coloured by the jealousy I am now feeling towards him.

My stomach tightens. I'd rush to tear them off, I'd even punch him if I could, but an invisible anchor holds me back. The image of my mother, her words reminding me not to act impulsively. Above all, not to make a fool of myself and get into trouble at such an important moment for me and the hotel. At least in this case, it's mainly my common sense, which, fortunately, I choose to listen to.

I peer out from behind a tall pot of pampas grass, but I can't hear anything. I see Evan saying something, while Arden lowers his gaze and his lips move slightly. Evan's smile broadens in a way I recognise even without having seen it on him before: the confident, triumphant kind that demands constant attention and gratitude, even if it eventually overwhelms you.

I step back a few paces so as not to be caught peeking too openly at them. From this vantage point, I can see Arden in profile. Evan touches his jacket sleeve, a gesture that seems private and intimate. Arden tries to withdraw, but Evan closes the gap, raising an arm to place his hand behind his neck, as if attempting to pull him into a hug. I notice, however, that the way Evan's thumb moves over that spot between Arden's neck and jaw seems more a sign of possession than affection.

I swallow and clench my fists. I have to try not to let my anger take over. He can touch him like this, obviously, but I can't. Then I'm gripped by a kind of fear, an anxiety I can't control. What if Arden wants it? What if that subtle bond, that understanding growing between us, doesn't truly exist? What if it's just a figment of my imagination, of my desire for him? I should move, but instead I stay still, so still that I don't notice Mars approaching.

'Hey, surfer, are you okay? You look as if you've just seen something truly dreadful! Am I wrong?'

I give him a tight smile and acknowledge it. Unfortunately, I can't do any better. I'm not that skilled at faking it.

'Nothing to report, actually.' I shrug, wary that I might not sound convincing.

Mars nods briefly, then frowns and glances towards the direction I was looking, sensing the tension and tightening his lips.

'That's why Arden went through hell last year. And even now, I honestly don't think he knows how to get rid of him, unfortunately. That guy is genuinely toxic.'

I listen to him, trying not to respond or overreact. This isn't the place, especially not the time, to try and intervene and cause a disaster.

Fortunately, Sarah's opening speech prevents me from acting impulsively, which I would have regretted. Everyone in the room is focused on the small wooden platform. I move to the appetiser table, pick up a glass of wine, and hold it between my fingers, trying to distract myself.

Sarah, very skilfully, speaks of *"resilient light, introspective narrative with profound meaning, rebirth as an act of freedom."* Every word she utters should make Arden proud of his work, but he still seems at Evan's mercy, as if he were subjugating him with his gestures, his gaze. I can sense it, even though I'm only watching them out of the corner of my eye. They both tilt their heads, arguing, and their faces are suddenly far too close.

Meanwhile, the evening unfolds amid applause and toasts. Arden finally manages to break free from Evan's grip and searches for me in the crowd. He spots me and approaches. I notice an apology in his slightly forced smile, even though he has no real reason to apologise.

'Hey... is everything okay?' he asks, but he seems to be the one having a problem.

I want to speak with him to truly share my thoughts. However, what comes out in a neutral tone feels cold and detached. Even though I act unconcerned, inside I cannot calm the current that surrounds me from head to toe.

'It is. What about you?' Suddenly I decide to take a risk, to go out on a limb. 'Is something wrong? Arden... you can talk to me about it if you want.'

Arden steps closer once more, then stops, shrugs, and shakes his head.

'It's complicated.'

He doesn't say anything else. His voice is low and tense. He only utters two simple words, but to me, they carry the weight of a thousand alarm bells. It takes less than a second for my rational side to give in to the protective instinct that kicks in during moments like these. However, I know I shouldn't interfere in situations that don't concern me. I also understand the influence Evan still wields over him.

'I was foolish enough to believe I could somehow be part of this "complication". But apparently, I was wrong.' The sentence escapes quickly, before I can stop it, and it's too abrupt. 'I'm sorry.'

I see him bite his lip and step back as if I've threatened to scratch him or, worse, hurt him deeply. Then I see him search for words to respond, but ultimately he gives up, narrows his eyes, and remains silent.

I'd like to say something, try to make amends somehow, but Sarah calls him over and invites him to join her for a photo for the local press. I follow him with my gaze for a moment, then try to look away. I need to maintain control, now more than ever.

I decide that distance is the only possible strategy in this situation. So, I walk towards the outdoor terrace, where the evening breeze briefly clears away the scents and voices. And, partly, also my resentment, the feeling of incompleteness that troubles me. I place my glass on the railing, no longer even wanting to drink. The sea refuses to give up, persistently employing that hypnotic undertow which usually has the power to soothe me. But tonight, unfortunately, it doesn't work. I find it intimidating, as if every wave is trying to remind me that nothing ever goes as I have hoped.

'A truly beautiful place, genuinely welcoming.' Evan Clarke's voice comes from behind me, relaxed and pleased. 'Congratulations.'

I don't need to turn around to know; I sense his confident smile before I see it. But I turn around anyway. Our gazes meet, his hazel eyes, seemingly warm, actually resemble two deadly weapons, poised to destroy.

'Thank you,' I reply, trying to keep my tone neutral and professional. Then I can't resist. 'Arden did an incredible job.'

He smiles faintly, with that arrogant expression that I now recognise as part of his character, part of his way of being and interacting with others.

'Arden always makes an effort to look his best when he's trying to impress someone who's wagging their tail around him.'

He knows exactly where to hit; he's truly a bloody bastard. He's intentionally trying to wind me up, it's clear. And he's succeeding, damn it!

'If you're here for him, to bother him in any way, just know that...'

'Oh, no.' He steps closer, then again, nearly invading my space. 'I'm here for you, Luke. I just want you to avoid investing too much in something... truly ephemeral.'

He tilts his head, as if willing to share a secret or offer friendly advice. Perhaps he doesn't realise that it would take very little to light the fuse about to explode inside me.

I lean against the railing. 'What are you implying?'

Evan raises his glass to his lips, sips slowly, then shrugs with the most innocent expression he can muster.

'About the fact that, even if you managed to get something out of him, it will never turn out the way you expect or want.' His words are slow and deliberate. But just cruel enough. 'Trust me, I know this from experience. I know him much better than you do. Arden is very good at running away when things get complicated or when situations escalate.'

I feel a scream, which I must hold back, resonate in my ribcage. Then a ringing in my ears, as if someone had suddenly turned down the volume on the rest of the world, leaving only Evan Clarke's words blaring in my head.

I don't respond. I can't. All the self-control I've learned over the years seems to vanish in the face of this individual. Yet, somehow, I manage to hold myself back, remaining still and silent as Evan walks away with the confidence of a judge who has just handed down his sentence.

When I breathe again, I reach for my glass, even though the desire to drink has truly passed. Or perhaps I need something decidedly stronger. Meanwhile, the night sea continues to crash against the shore, indifferent to my turmoil. But I feel the current changing course right beneath my skin, ready to take away every hold, every hope of achieving something beautiful in this life, something true. Something akin to happiness.

CHAPTER 7

Arden

In the days following my "misunderstanding" with Luke, which mainly arose from Evan's presence and my overall tension, things seemed to have settled between us. In fact, we've avoided discussing it altogether, as if the incident never occurred. We've shared other pleasant moments on the beach, sometimes with Sarah, Mars, and the others. We haven't truly become close, at least not as much as I'd like, but we haven't grown apart either. We're still in a "friendly" phase, often touching each other, but it's as if neither of us dares to go too far, and for now, I'd say that's okay. I certainly don't want to rush things and risk ruining everything.

I'm also very busy with work, so I try to stay calm and focused to perform at my best. I want everything to be perfect; this assignment is really important to me and could be a turning point in my career.

The others, however, are also helping to make this event memorable. Today, for example, the veranda of the High Tide looks as if it has been transformed into a 1950s film set. The ivory tablecloths are perfectly ironed, the silver flatware gleams brightly, and enormous windows frame the coastline like a living painting. I, to be honest, feel almost like an insider with my wrinkled jacket and distressed expression. It seems the morning coffee had no effect on me, as it didn't quite wake me up.

Luke, wearing a pale blue shirt with his sleeves carefully rolled up, waits at the entrance. His stiff posture makes it seem as if he's been compelled to memorise a script and is now reviewing it to avoid making mistakes.

Then I see her. From the way she's been described to me over the past few days, announcing her arrival, it's unquestionably her. Jocelyn Whitaker enters with the authority of a high court judge, dressed in a cream-coloured suit, pearl necklace, and perfectly styled blonde hair despite the humidity. Meanwhile, she wafts a strong gardenia scent that reminds me of certain Midwestern spaces. Her blue eyes, a hue very similar to Luke's, scan the entrance and then the room, as if measuring lines and streaks of invisible dust. When they meet mine, a question seems to flash through her mind but remains unspoken.

Perhaps because I'm observing her as if I know her.

Luke, meanwhile, moves towards her.

'Mom, welcome to High Tide.'

He kisses her on the cheek, and his smile radiates a strange confidence, as if the situation is entirely under control. Maybe for him, it genuinely is.

'It's truly lovely, honey.' Jocelyn twists her body to glance around quickly. 'It smells like...' she sniffs the air, raises an eyebrow. 'Like what, exactly?'

'Black fig beeswax. Homemade formula.' Luke replies, his voice sounding a couple of tones higher than usual. I'm not even sure if he's serious or just kidding.

They look in my direction and our eyes meet, so he feels compelled to approach, and she follows. He introduces me to his mother, barely glancing at me.

'Mom, this is Arden Morales, the guest photographer for the festival.'

Just "guest photographer," then. No mention of anything else — of the friendship, the connection between us, the fun we've had these past few days, the work we've done together, the moments we've shared, or the reflections on light and shadow. Everything else, in short.

I feel a bit silly, in a way. But then again, what did I expect? That he'd introduce me to his mother as... as something I can't even define yet?

But inside me, I feel a warning bell ringing, warning me: *"Don't get too involved in this. You might get hurt."* Likewise, I feel my stomach tighten, but I reach out, trying to hide my true thoughts.

'Nice to meet you, Mrs. Whitaker.'

Jocelyn gives me a firm squeeze and offers a polite, yet rather indifferent, smile.

'How wonderful to have an artist among us. Art always adds... a certain colour.'

I find the pause between "always" and "colour" quite meaningful. Enough to make me picture a stain on fine fabric. Like me, at the moment, I feel like a small decorative feature.

I've been invited to lunch, as if I were an important collaborator, along with Sarah and Mars. I try to remain calm and relaxed as Jocelyn talks about her trip, the airport, the overly lively young people, and the alternative foods sold at the kiosks. I realise that, despite her conversation with a kind of tender condescension, every sentence radiates prejudice and even a certain detachment towards anything she considers to be outside her "rules".

I don't want to be prejudiced, but I notice that Luke also looks uncomfortable. I respond in monosyllables to try to hide my true thoughts, while Sarah and Mars fortunately manage to be spontaneous and liven up the conversation.

After lunch, Luke suggests going on a boat trip, perhaps to ease the tension a bit.

'It's the best view of the cliffs and the ArtWave coastal installations.'

Actually, I understand his intentions. He's seeking a neutral setting where the ocean can serve as a backdrop to the awkwardness that might emerge with his mother, along with the discomfort that has sadly arisen after Evan's unexpected appearance.

If I followed my instincts, I would walk away and find refuge alone, but instead I accept because I don't want to complicate things between us or between him and his mother.

When we set sail, Luke is at the helm of the motorboat, Jocelyn is sitting on the bow with Sarah talking about fashion, and I'm at the stern with Mars and Jack, who is calmly lounging, enjoying the pleasant breeze.

The sea is a gently rippled blue mirror. At one point, Sarah points out to Jocelyn some of the murals on the cliffs. Among the other images are rainbow flags with meaningful slogans about love, the importance of resistance, and the freedom to choose how to live and whom to love.

I notice Jocelyn's eyes narrow slightly, then her brow furrows, before that familiar smug smile appears on her rosy lips.

'Very expressive, I'd say,' she comments. Then, she turns to me: 'I imagine a bohemian artist like you would be comfortable in this colourful environment. Will it stimulate your... fantasies?'

That attitude again. That condescending yet, at the same time, slightly contemptuous tone. I feel myself flushing. I must try to hold back, I know!

'I'd say it's about truth rather than fantasy. Art gives voice to those who are often forced into silence or judged superficially, without even making the effort to understand their personal experiences.' I don't raise my voice; I stay calm, but each word I utter reflects the disappointment I feel at this moment. 'You can't remain silent in the face of abuse.'

Jocelyn smiles before adjusting her scarf around her neck. 'Oh, my dear, silence isn't always the enemy. Sometimes it's elegance. And sometimes remaining silent is the best choice.'

'With all due respect, ma'am, certain elegances are only comfortable for those who can afford them.'

Luke gives me a pleading look, almost panicked. I understand what he's asking. He wants me to stop arguing with his mother. So, essentially, like her, he's imposing silence on me. The same silence he's adopted for several years, I imagine.

He feigns to examine the compass dial before calling his mother's attention.

'Mom, look at that sea cave over there!' He tries to engage her in another topic of conversation.

I bite my tongue, unwilling to cause further discomfort. Still, I feel uneasy. Anyway, Luke's ploy doesn't appear to be working because his mother is stubbornly determined to have the last word.

'I understand, Arden. It's natural for young people to want to try... expressing themselves. Just remember not to impose your rainbow on those who prefer more sober hues.'

I have a feeling the boat lurched the moment Luke let go of the helm for a second.

'The "more sober hues" you mention often resemble paint hiding a crack,' I reply firmly. Luke might be angry with me now, but it doesn't matter. 'And I search for cracks in my work.'

At my words, Jocelyn's eyes narrow until they resemble two slender blades.

'Interesting theory, young man. I hope you don't intend to include family issues in your subjects.'

Sarah and Mars, usually chatty, remained silent, listening to the overly lively exchange between Jocelyn and me. Or perhaps they don't dare intervene in a conversation they feel is a bit too complex and thorny.

Luke finally intervenes, and I realise there's no point in arguing with his mother any further. 'Can we enjoy the view now?'

I sense his tension and realise that the conversation between Luke and Jocelyn has been ongoing, perhaps for quite some time. And it will remain so forever unless Luke decides to speak openly with his mother about his sexual orientation.

Meanwhile, through a strange twist of fate, the clouds seem to gather, and the sea becomes choppy.

Jocelyn wrinkles her nose in displeasure. 'They didn't predict rain today.'

As if to contradict her, the first drop hits the wood with a dry sound, followed by more and more. Within minutes, the rain begins to pour harder, and the waves also rise violently around the boat.

Luke orders firmly: 'Everyone inside, quickly!'

Jocelyn takes refuge in the cabin, followed by Sarah and Mars. Jack slips behind them. I, however, remain motionless on the deck, needing to catch my breath and be alone for a moment, despite the rain.

When a stronger gust hurls icy water against my chest, Luke goes to close the cabin door, then returns and grabs my arm.

'Get down!' he shouts.

'I'm going.' But meanwhile, I stay still.

'You don't understand, Arden. I'm not suggesting this.' He tightens his grip on my arm, but I still refuse to obey his request. Or his order, whatever it is.

'I understand.' More water hits us, hitting us both. 'Just as I understand something else.'

I understand that if I want a chance with him, I must be deluded.

I understand that Luke will never take any action to alter his circumstances.

I understand, above all, that I shouldn't get involved in this... except that I am already involved! More than I would like.

I see his lips quiver, not so much from the rain or fear, but from restrained anger.

'You can't defy my mother, Arden. You don't know her; you'll never win against her.'

'I didn't defy her, Luke. I was just standing up for myself and what I believe in. Which, perhaps, you should start doing too, one day.'

A crash of thunder interrupts us, the boat nearly lifts as it hits a wave, and I, unsteady, risk falling. But Luke keeps me upright.

'So many details of my life would hurt her.' His voice trembles, and I sense his torment. 'I almost lost her once, when my father left for another woman and I decided to live my own life. I can't risk that happening again. I can't tell her the truth, at least not entirely. Not yet. It would be like betraying her again.'

I nod and place my hand on his arm. I understand, more than he thinks, even if it's not easy for me to accept. He talks about emptiness, the terror of being alone, rootless.

'But you, Luke? What will happen to you? Should you remain "invisible" to avoid hurting what she believes in, or to prevent offending her sensibilities?'

I'm not talking about myself, but it's obvious that I am part of the "picture" that Luke isn't yet willing to reveal. The issue is that, by going along with it, I risk remaining just a detail and enduring more suffering.

'I'm not invisible, Arden,' he replies, shaking his head. 'And neither are you. Not to me.'

Another wave, even larger, crashes onto the bridge. This time, however, spotting it approaching, I grip the railing and manage to stay steady.

'Luke, I've already tolerated a man who demanded I disappear so as not to disturb anyone. Evan has always overwhelmed me with his personality. I won't go through that kind of situation again, for anyone in the world.'

Luke's eyes darken, almost matching the colour of the stormy sky above us.

'I'm not asking you that. I...' He pauses, then takes a deep breath as if starving for air. 'I'm scared, Arden. I'm scared of severing the bond with my mother forever, but at the same time... I'm scared of losing myself, who I truly am, who I want to be.'

The wind now seems almost howling, growing stronger. But during a moment of apparent respite, at least between us, I place my hand on his chest, at the level of his heart. I feel it pounding wildly.

'No one is asking you to decide who you love, Luke. You don't have to choose me, I hope that's clear.' My words come out shaky, perhaps, but honest. 'I only ask you not to deny anything.'

Luke nods and closes his eyes, then places his hand on mine, which I hold against his chest.

Finally, he rests his forehead against mine. Our ragged breaths mingle as raindrops run down our faces and lips.

'Okay, Arden. Can you go below decks now, please?' He looks at me with a determined expression. 'I don't like seeing you in danger.'

I nod and roll my eyes, then offer a faint smile.

'All right, Captain.'

When the wind dies down, we decide to turn back. Luke moves to steer the boat towards the shore through the whitecaps of the waves. At the same time, I choose to stop defying his mother and give him some time to figure out what he truly wants from me and from his life.

As the shore appears on the horizon, I step out onto the deck and try to relax a bit. The rain has nearly stopped, though the sky remains dark, so dark it feels like a sheet of lead overhead.

And that's exactly when it happens. I can see him clearly and make him out on the nearby shore now, standing on the wooden walkway. He's behind a telescopic tripod, with a telephoto lens aimed at our boat. Unmistakable, with broad shoulders and dark hair slicked back.

Evan.

I catch a glimpse of his satisfied smile as he turns away from the camera to look directly at me. So I see him work again. Another click, which I clearly feel I can hear, even over the roar of the waves. Then darkness returns inside me. My heart spirals, like a whirlwind I can't control. That man has just captured Luke's boat returning to shore. He knows how to use images like blades. And he's ready to strike. Because, knowing Evan, I know he has something diabolical and perverse in mind.

I grip the rope tightly until my knuckles turn white. I hear Luke shout my name from the top of the ladder. Luckily, he doesn't seem to have noticed Evan. I want to answer him, but it's as if I can't speak because of the lump in my throat that's holding me back. I feel swallowed by another storm, not of water and wind, but of destructive memories. And fear returns to me. Fear of becoming the property of someone who would use any means to keep me caged. Fear of sinking into another abyss of despair. And of never being able to climb back out.

CHAPTER 8

Luke

No alarm clock can compete with the mix of guilt and fear gnawing at me. At dawn, in my apartment, I'm still tossing and turning in bed, unable to find a moment's peace. On the nightstand, my phone flashes with notifications I don't dare open. I've returned from the boat trip after the storm that hit us, with my mother strangely silent and distracted, and Arden, who, as soon as we reached the dock, muttered, "I have some matters to take care of myself" before disappearing straight to his suite— or so I think. And yet, I thought he understood!

Jack, always very sensitive to my mood swings, yelps softly and lifts his large eyes to me, scrutinising me questioningly. I reach out and run a hand over his back.

'My bad, mate. I always seem to mess up my life and turn it into a complete disaster.'

Resigned to my lack of sleep, I decide to get up and dress quickly. I might as well get some work done.

Before eight, I meet Raphael in the lobby, who gives me a summary of the night: no damage, the guests are quiet and have no special requests. Only the guest in Suite 3 has asked not to be disturbed under any circumstances.

Suite 3… Arden. A lump in my throat tightens.

I should simply grant his request and leave him alone; that would be the easiest solution. But I can't, so I head straight for his room.

I knock, first with two gentle taps, then more insistently. Only later do I realise the time. Perhaps he's still asleep and I'm disturbing him. But I can't even explain why; the thought doesn't really cross my mind. I knock again, a little louder. Then, I actually call out to him.

'Arden?'

No answer. But a rather bright light is filtering through the crack under the door, so he's probably awake. Or he's in a very deep sleep. Or maybe he's working; perhaps he's editing some photos.

I wait a few more moments, then I give up and walk away. I realise that maybe he truly wants to be left alone.

I need to apologise, talk to him, and resolve the situation between us. I have to do it quickly, or I risk regretting it forever. I can't live in suspense any longer, and above all, I can't lose him, and myself, in the process.

By midday, the lobby is already crowded with people, yet Arden is nowhere to be seen. I begin to worry more. Despite our differences, it's odd that he hasn't left his room, unless he seized some moment I was distracted to slip away and avoid a confrontation. I need to find out what's happening, especially with the festival nearing its peak and new guests arriving specifically for the event.

This is exactly what I'm trying to focus on: the ArtWave. Meanwhile, Sarah is coordinating the workers assembling a glass walkway on the observation deck for the upcoming gala. I'm helping to check some cables when Evan materialises near the reception and fixes his gaze on me, as if ready to challenge me. He's wearing a white shirt and his camera is slung around his neck. Since he's not staying at the High Tide, I was harbouring the vain hope that he'd left and was no longer in the area. I was obviously deluding myself.

I dislike the fact that he's wandering around the hotel undisturbed, but with the event scheduled, I can't remove him; I'd risk causing a fuss that might backfire on me. However, maybe that's exactly what he wants!

'Do you have a minute?' He approaches me and speaks in that tone which, in any case, brooks no refusal. 'I need to talk to you.'

I nod, mainly to get him off my back, and I persuade him to follow me into a service room. When we arrive, Evan lowers his head as if sharing a secret and slips a black USB drive between my fingers.

'What is it?' I ask, feeling unconvinced.

I like this man less and less. In fact, saying "I like him less and less" is an understatement. He's absolutely driving me mad, and it has nothing to do with the fact that he was with Arden, nor that he might even manage to get back together, sooner or later.

'Inside is evidence of how Arden is… less of a victim than he appears, let's say.' He smiles, shrugging with a pompous, commanding expression. 'Videos, chats, and various images. I assure you, there's enough to shatter the sob story of the artist who endured so much suffering, who seeks beauty amid the desolation of this life. However, if you truly care and want to prevent them from circulating during the grand gala, I have a simple request: include me in the main programme with a performance of my own, during the prime-time slot. Of course, as for the material on Arden, I provided you… You can study it and keep it as a keepsake; I have other copies. And while we're at it… the story between you and my boyfriend makes no sense, you understand that too, right? I advise you not to delve any further.'

I can hardly understand what this creep is saying to me. I only know that the blood is starting to boil in my veins, reaching my temples.

'This is blackmail. I don't mean...'

'No, blackmail! What an unpleasant word. It's simply a negotiation between professionals.' Evan interrupts me, flashing his devilish grin. Then he opens his arms with a candour that's clearly not his own. 'Anyway, you still have some time. Make your choice. But I advise you to first look at the material I've given you. Then you can decide freely!'

Freely, he says? This man is a monster, a slimy manipulator, yet somehow sensual and charming. I wonder how Arden could have been with him, blast it!

I stand frozen as Evan Clarke turns his back on me and walks away. Even though it's impossible, I have the distinct sensation of the metal of the USB flash drive burning my palm. Part of me wants to throw it to the ground and destroy it, then chase

Evan and punch him until I wipe that evil smile off his face. The other part knows I might be holding something that could compromise Arden or even ruin him. And whatever it is, I don't want that.

I want to understand and support him if I can. I trust him, so I'm almost certain he hasn't done anything wrong. But I need to discover what he's concealing and then try to free him from Evan Clarke's evil influence. Once and for all.

CHAPTER 9

Luke

In an effort to find a solution, I retreated to my office. Despite my reluctance, I was compelled to insert the USB drive Evan gave me into my computer and browse through the materials he has against Arden.

That's how I realised the situation. Intimate and personal photos of Arden, along with moments of suffering, anxiety, and panic attacks. I can't believe that bastard has gone this far in the past and is now willing to carry out his threats.

I try to consider what to do, then I send a message to Mars and Sarah, asking them both to join me as soon as possible. I need the help of someone who is at least partly aware of what Arden went through with that monster.

Ten minutes later, Mars shows up, dressed in his casual clothes and holding a coffee. Sarah arrives right after him and looks at us with a puzzled expression.

I update them on what has happened, or at least I try, aiming to remain as calm as possible. Then I show them the flash drive without inserting it into the computer. I don't want them to see the material Evan wants to use against Arden; they'll have to take my word for it, at least for now.

Mars emits a sharp whistle, then rolls his eyes.

'This is outright blackmail. And to do it, that jerk is exploiting Arden's trauma. It's typical. And I might add, it's characteristic of Evan Clarke. His way of removing rivals and competitors who are better than him has always been to publicly discredit them. But now he's doing it privately too, and it's even more revolting!'

Sarah nods and confirms Mars's words.

'If it indeed contains sensitive material, releasing it could destroy Arden more than it has already armed him. It would ruin him both professionally and personally. We must stop him, one way or another.'

I watch them. I don't know what they're up to, but I know they're more experienced than I am in situations like these, especially in handling the audience and diverting attention elsewhere.

Mars crosses his arms and tilts his head for a moment. Then, suddenly, he appears to perk up and claps his hands eagerly.

'We could organise a kind of performative flash mob. We'll make him think we're at his disposal, but instead we'll steal the spotlight from Evan so that his "weapon" against Arden becomes his downfall.'

I look at him, confused. I can't understand what he means. But Sarah, apparently, is more perceptive than I am, because she nods confidently. Then she opens the event map.

'It's not a bad idea at all; I think it could work. We have about twenty minutes between the live painting and the main screening. If, before Evan starts his performance, we turn that interval into a collective act that reveals his tricks and modus operandi, his "truth" will turn into a farce before he even considers executing it against Arden.'

'I get it, guys.' At least, I think I do. I'm not an artist, and I'm feeling quite confused now. Maybe it's the pressure I'm under. 'But how do you plan to put this idea into practice?'

Mars, unexpectedly and with an almost feline leap, springs up from his chair.

'Easy enough, surfer! All walls are screens, every wound is a project of light!' he recites, with his usual emphasis. Then he descends and darkens his gaze, becoming serious again. 'We'll use Evan's same material, the one he's always used against his opponents, reworking it against him. It won't be difficult to track down the people he's hurt over the course of his miserable career. I'm sure they'll be on our side. Even what he has against Arden, avoiding the most traumatic and compromising situations, of course. Obviously, we'll have to pretend to agree to that wretch's demands, so he falls into our trap.'

'But for this, we'll have to involve Arden as well,' Sarah adds. 'He can't be kept in the dark about our plans, or he might risk ruining everything if he faces Evan directly. And that's down to you, Luke. In fact, I suggest you keep Arden as far away from that psychopath as possible, if you can.'

A ray of hope offers a little light and seems to ease my sense of guilt. However, I harbour some doubts about Arden's involvement in the enterprise.

'Arden won't trust me easily. Not after...' I sigh and shake my head, feeling disheartened.

Not after our discussion, where he pressured me into making a decision I didn't feel comfortable with.

Sarah gives me a dark, almost resentful look.

'Then you must make him trust you. Only you can do that; that'll be your job. We'll handle the rest. But you need to do it as soon as possible so I can programme the projectors for the reworked images and Mars can arrange the text.'

The determination in their expressions and words is like a slap in the face to my doubts, my inertia.

I can't help but agree to their request.

'Alright, I understand. I will do my part.'

***

I spend most of the afternoon organising the installation, replying to guests' messages, and pretending everything is normal with my mother as she wanders around the hotel, commenting on the bad weather as a sign of "divine displeasure with artistic extravagance." I resist snapping at her. In fact, I try not to hear her. I don't want to have a discussion like this, not right now. But as soon as I can, I'll need to reach a clear understanding, even with her.

As the sky begins to take on the usual hues of sunset, the veranda empties. Most of the artists present go to dine in town. I head for the pier, carrying the USB flash drive Evan gave me. I wish

I could throw it into the sea and make it vanish forever, but I can't. It is tangible proof of his threat. And it is precisely under his own threats that Evan Clarke will have to fall and answer for all his misdeeds, both professional and personal.

Late that evening, I decide to cross the third-floor corridor and reach Suite 3. The door is closed, but the soft lights filter through the crack, and I hear movement inside. As if Arden were working on a video. I knock softly and wait. No response, as I expected. I'm tempted to give up and retreat, but I don't want to surrender this time. I knock again, with more force and determination.

Ten seconds pass, and in the meantime, silence settles inside. Perhaps he's decided to wait for the person at the door to choose to leave. Instead, I hear the click of the lock. Arden appears, wearing a black T-shirt, with deep bags under his eyes and a look that seems caught between desolation and exhaustion. Behind him, I catch a glimpse of the computer monitor showing a silent sequence of black-and-white shots: cracks, water, waves, lightning.

My heart starts pounding.

'I need you to listen to me, Arden.'

Silence. Then a deep sigh. He nods once. He holds the door open but doesn't let me in, standing in the threshold, creating a sort of boundary between us.

'Okay.' He says nothing more.

I take a breath, knowing I must be convincing and earn his trust, despite everything.

'There's something we need to do tomorrow. It's important, and we must do it together. Evan is trying to hurt you, as he has done to others before. But with you...' I'm not sure how to carry on; his gaze makes me believe he knows about the situation and Evan's blackmail. He knows him, after all. Much better than I do, and for much longer. 'We can turn his wicked game around, Arden. We mustn't give in or even succumb to his manipulations. I have no intention of allowing that, anyway. I have a plan with Sarah and Mars, but for it to succeed... I need you to trust me in the next few hours. Completely.'

His amber eyes narrow on me, as if measuring the gap between what I ask of him and what I deserve. I notice his hands trembling, then he clenches his fists to hold himself back.

'Why should I?' he whispers, shrugging. He looks utterly resigned, as if he desperately wants to give up. 'I've always had to deal with Evan's manipulation and abuse; I'm used to it now. He always wins; there's nothing you can do to stop him once he sets his mind on something. And you...

Since our last discussion, it didn't seem like you were very willing to expose yourself. So, in the end...'

So, in the end, am I really that different from his ex? Is that what he's trying to tell me? My silence, my urge to hide, has caused him pain—perhaps a different kind of pain, but pain all the same.

'Because this time I'm asking you, or rather, I'm begging you, to trust me. This time, I don't intend to hide, Arden. In fact, not just this time!' I place a hand on his chest, then grasp his arm, trying to draw him closer. 'Let me prove it to you. Give me a chance.'

Arden keeps his eyes fixed on mine before lowering his gaze to the floor. At last, he looks back at me. Still uncertain, I sense that, in his mind and heart, a struggle between emotion and reason is occurring.

'All right, Luke.' He nods, lightly biting his lower lip. 'If you care that much, I'll give you a chance.'

I'm tempted to grab him, kiss him, push him into his room, and genuinely show him how I feel. But for now, there's a more urgent matter to attend to — removing that worm Evan Clarke from his life once and for all.

'Thank you.'

I won't say anything more. Maybe because that's the only word that makes sense between us right now. As for everything else, I can only hope.

I hope Mars and Sarah's plan truly works. I hope Evan falls into our trap. I hope the truth prevails, as it should. I hope things go well between me and Arden. I hope I can build a happy life for myself. I hope I can finally be true to myself—without any more doubts, suffering, or misunderstandings.

Without hiding any longer.

CHAPTER 10

Arden

It's early in the morning when Luke knocks on my door again. In the hours after his visit, I haven't been able to sleep much. I've kept focusing on work for the final ArtWave presentation and have been lost in my thoughts, which mostly revolve around him and the opportunity he's asked me to give him.

I've kept a certain distance from him, I realise. But I'm afraid to let go, afraid to delude myself. Yet I couldn't help it because the truth is, I'm even more afraid of ending up in a situation where I'll have to regret it forever.

Once I open the door, I look into his grey-blue eyes, which have never appeared so resolute and determined. This time, he doesn't seem to have the slightly lost look of someone asking for permission, but rather that of someone willing to do anything to achieve his goals, including stealing time and space from destiny. He's wearing light jeans, a black T-shirt, and a light jacket. His blond hair is slightly messy, with uneven locks.

'You're an early riser...' I mutter, still in my boxers and T-shirt.

'I know.' He sighs and lifts a container with two coffees. 'This is to help you wake up. Anyway, I have something special in mind, you won't regret it. Put on something, we're leaving!'

'We're leaving where? Luke, are you mad? Do you realise that leaving now is completely unwise? Do you realise that the final presentation at High Tide is tomorrow?'

'I completely understand that! That's exactly why I have something special in mind.' He smiles and nods confidently. 'I promise I won't waste your valuable time, and your presentation won't suffer. Besides, you've been working too many hours, locked in here. I'm sure you've prepared it down to the last detail by now. It's time to go out and get some fresh air; it can only do you good!'

I want to refuse and even tell him to go to hell. But the truth is, I can't resist him. I can't resist those bright eyes of his that now seem so sincere. I can't resist his deep voice, his muscular, seductive body that attracts me like no one else, not even Evan.

I still don't know whether to call it kidnapping, escaping, or a leap into the unknown. I only know that, when he passes me the hot coffee and brushes my face with his free hand, without taking his eyes off mine, I feel I have no other choice. Something inside me decides that I can trust him and that I must give him a chance. Otherwise, I really risk regretting him for the rest of my life.

I sip my coffee and quickly change into a clean T-shirt and a pair of jeans. I pack my backpack, including my camera. Jack, who had followed Luke to my room, wags his tail behind us until his owner hands him over to Raphael, promising double the cuddles and treats upon our return.

'Are you ready for a spectacular journey?' Luke asks, challenging me with a confident look.

'At this point, I'm not backing down.' I accept the challenge; I can't help myself. 'I'm ready!'

CHAPTER 11

Arden

It's only 7:30 a.m. and we're on Highway 101. The slanting light of early morning casts pink streaks on the cliffs and billboards. Luke drives with his elbow resting on the open window, the radio tuned to an old country music programme. Every now and then, he taps his fingers on the steering wheel, keeping time, and I watch as if captivated by his gestures. Meanwhile, I take every opportunity to snap quick shots of the landscape and its outline illuminated by the reflection of the light.

At one point, he suddenly stops and turns to look at me askance.

'You're taking photos of me while I'm driving. I can't figure out what you're seeing.'

'Relax, it's not your job to figure anything out right now.'

He shakes his head and laughs. The sound of his laughter dispels my dark thoughts from yesterday.

And he pushes the paranoia from my mind, our argument about his mother, and Evan's threats. Everything else that pulls us into a vortex of impatience that has nothing to do with us.

I try to relax and enjoy the moment until we reach our destination. Santa Ynez welcomes us with its rolling hills, the air smelling of damp earth and wild rosemary. Luke parks beside a barn that looks like it's been turned into an elegant winery, or rather, a wine boutique as the sign describes it.

A tall man wearing a straw hat and a friendly smile approaches us. His name is Morris. I learn that he's a college friend of Luke's, now a biodynamic winemaker. He hands us a basket overflowing with food, including warm focaccia, olives, and a couple of bottles of rosé.

'Take the pickup, guys. It's already loaded with wood, and there are blankets and sweaters. It might be chilly.'

Ten minutes later, we jump into the creaking seats of a cream-coloured vintage Chevy and drive up a dirt track towards the top of the hill. Far from the spotlights, the anxiety of the ArtWave presentation, and everything else, the world seems to shrink within our borders. So, it's just the two of us and a horizon that finally feels like we can breathe.

When we reach our destination, Luke unloads the wood near a circle of rocks. I lend him a hand and then retrieve the windproof lighter I keep for my creative emergencies. As the first flames rise up the logs, I grab my Nikon from my backpack. I want to try to capture, in a photograph, the flame colouring his cheeks at this moment, the slightly tense line of his smile as he tries to find the courage to express himself, to let go.

But we remain mostly silent, as if neither of us dares to intrude into the other's personal space. We drink the wine Morris has placed in the basket in tin glasses, watching the flames flicker in the fire before us. The silence hums, filled with what we need to say but haven't yet dared to voice.

Ultimately, Luke is the first to break the ice.

'I'm sorry about what happened during lunch and the boat ride. My mother isn't quite what she seems to be. I mean... she is, really. But I think she's mainly afraid. After my father's sudden abandonment, she's clung to certain rules, especially concerning me. Everything should go according to her plan, with no further upheavals. And this... well, being who I am is definitely an upheaval for her. It's as if I, like my father, sabotage her plans. When, during college, I told her I was in a serious relationship with Keith, a man, she gave me a strange, almost hysterical smile. Then she locked herself in her room and refused to talk about it anymore. As if, by avoiding direct confrontation, she could remove what she disliked and couldn't accept. As if I could change... or heal, according to her. Simply by avoiding discussing it, as if the "problem" didn't exist.'

I nod and sigh at his words. I understand, even though my parents accepted my choices with more calm. I was lucky, at least in that aspect.

'I'd never seen her break down,' Luke continues. 'Not even when my father left her to go off with his young assistant. So, aside from a few texts in which I tried to rekindle the conversation, I never spoke to her about it again. Then, anyway, my relationship with Keith ended. After that, I had a few flings — nothing noteworthy. And obviously, when I moved here for work, I avoided letting her know about my love life.'

I carry on listening to him, without interrupting. Luke takes a sip and gazes into the fire for a moment. Then a look exchanged between us prompts him to continue.

'When she called you a "bohemian artist", I saw that closed door again. I realised that the same threat was probably recurring for her, and I reacted by trying to control the situation, to block out the "threat". Except that what is a threat to her represents the most alive part of me, to me. What I am, what I want to be.'

I bite my lip, close my eyes briefly, and then clear my throat.

'As far as I'm concerned, there were never any closed doors with Evan. In fact, he always left them open so he could come in whenever he wanted and act undisturbed, manipulating my ideas and my self-esteem. Initially, everything felt simple and wonderful. There was passion, creativity, and joint effort. Everything was fine, until... until I began achieving greater success and, as a result, more opportunities than he did. Evan couldn't stand that, just as he's never been able to stand people who succeed in achieving goals denied to him. He reacts with hatred, with anger... even with blackmail, if necessary. And even though I refused to admit it at the time, this side of his character has always unsettled me. Since I was his partner, the situation worsened. He started criticising every success I had, belittling my work, and even despising me as a person. As if there was truly nothing commendable about me or what I created. Not to him, at least. And I... I trusted him, his judgment, but he corrupted my trust to the point of psychologically destroying me. At twenty-nine, he made me feel like a nobody, in every sense. As if all the goals I had achieved were pointless. Then... he resorted to physical violence. And even then, he always claimed that people would believe him, not me.'

Luke narrows his eyes at me, touches my left arm, and traces it until he reaches my wrist, then places his index finger on my scar, which he'd already noticed that evening on the beach.

'This is from when I first tried to leave his house. Ethan threw a glass to the ground, and then, with a glass...'

Luke squirms in place and lets out a guttural sound, like a scream bursting from within him. He pulls back his hair, holds it with one hand, then lets it fall.

'If I see him coming in again, I won't answer for myself.'

I shake my head. 'No, Luke, I don't want revenge. That's not why I'm telling you everything. I want... I want air, I want to breathe again. Now that you're here with me, in this enchanting place, in front of the fire... I want to remember that I'm not broken, that despite the pain Evan has imprinted inside me, the marks he's left on my skin, he hasn't been able to destroy me.'

Luke envelops me in his embrace, and a silence, now almost surreal, prevails between us. Only the crackling of the embers punctuates our heartbeats.

Then he smiles, lifts the bottle of wine, and narrows his eyes.

'What shall we toast, Arden?'

'To the light that keeps resisting, even through the cracks? Or to the light among the waves, while you were teaching me to surf?'

'To both, I would say.'

Luke nods, pours the remaining wine, and we toast by clinking our glasses. As the liquid slides down my throat, I truly feel that our toast marks the end of something... and the beginning of a new cycle in our lives.

When I lower my glass, Luke turns fully towards me. He's even closer, so much so that I feel his chest almost against mine. His pupils reflect the flames, two dark blue mirrors on a place I don't yet know well but that I'm beginning to recognise as home.

'Can I...?' The question lingers between us, like glowing embers. Meanwhile, Luke gently strokes my cheek with his fingers, tilting his head slightly.

I don't answer his question; I surrender immediately. It's just the slightest movement on my part. I let myself drift towards him, and he instantly realises and leans even closer, wrapping his arms around my hips. Meanwhile, I savour his breath, his breath that, unknowingly, helps bring back to life scattered pieces of my soul, fragments of my heart that I had thought were destroyed forever.

When our lips finally meet and our tongues intertwine, I feel a jolt of electricity that grips me completely, from my heels to my scalp. As if every unfinished detail finds its place on his skin, in his arms. Meanwhile, his warm hands move to the nape of my neck to pull me even closer, and mine encircle his chest, as if I feared he would slip away from me at any moment. But Luke has no intention of leaving, he has no intention of moving away, and I feel his heart beating in unison with mine.

We part with a sigh, almost with difficulty, but we stay with our bodies entwined, even a little breathless, as if we've run a course to cross a boundary that, until recently, we hadn't dared to face.

So, in each other's arms, amidst kisses and whispers, we share everything. Truly everything—past and present. Including Evan's blackmail, the compromising images of me he possesses, and Sarah and Mars's plan to banish him from our lives forever.

'If you think this is a good idea...' I look him in the eyes, intertwining my fingers with his. 'Luke, I would never want to cause problems or inconvenience to you and the hotel, especially now, in the midst of ArtWave. Maybe I could talk to Evan, reach a compromise with him, and persuade him to...'

'No, Arden.' Luke's gaze darkens, and I see sparks of tension and implacable fury in his eyes. 'I meant it when I said Evan shouldn't come near you again. He would seize the chance to hurt you once more; we both know that.'

'Yes, you're right.' I'm forced to admit it. But I still don't want Luke and the guys to risk anything to protect me.

'I asked you to trust me. Can you do that, Arden?'

He smiles and runs his finger along my cheekbone, then tilts his face slightly to kiss me on the lips with a passion that takes my breath away.

'Okay.' I roll my eyes and look for his mouth again. 'You're quite convincing, I must say.'

'I'm glad.' He wrinkles his nose in satisfaction. 'And as for my mother... I'll talk to her before the event. And she'll have to understand this time.'

'Don't force things, Luke.' I rest my head on his shoulder. 'I'm sure she'll understand, but it might take some time...'

Whatever happens, I'm glad to see him so confident and determined. It's not just about me, about us, or about our story that's yet to be born and that I hope will grow over time. It's about him, about who he truly is, and about what he wants for himself and his life. About his essence, his feelings, which, from now on, he will no longer need to hide or deny.

When we decide to go back, even if reluctantly, we feel safer and undeniably closer. I tune the radio to an '80s music station and follow the beat, nodding my head. Luke reaches out his hand and interlocks his fingers with mine. He drives with his other hand, as if it were the most natural thing in the world. The warmth of his palm sparks a fire in my chest. I long to hold him, to kiss him again, to move forward, but there will be time for that. Our priorities are different now.

We return the pickup to Morris and set off again. When we reach High Tide, everything appears quite peaceful. We get into the lift together, heading to my room, and we kiss once more. Luke pushes me against the wall and presses his body against mine.

'Try to rest, even just a little,' he sighs against my lips before I go down to my suite. 'In the meantime, I'll talk to my mother. Then, in the late afternoon, we'll start the first screenings and the plan the guys have devised. That way, Evan will fall, along with all his scheming.'

I smile and glance at him, leaning in to kiss him again before the elevator doors close. I step into my room, take off my shirt, and collapse onto the bed.

Following Luke's advice, I'm about to close my eyes and surrender to sleep, but my phone vibrates in my pocket. Notifications come from Instagram, WhatsApp, and even Messenger. The sender is unknown, but I recognise it instantly.

The initial message is a photograph accompanied by a highly accurate description.

"You and me, two years ago, shirtless, light from the window, bites on the chest. Evan Clarke – The Real Vision."

The second message is even more disturbing, at least to me. It shows Luke and me laughing in the water after surfing. The description is simply two words: *"New trophy?"* in white letters.

The third message is a link. I click on it. It's an unfamiliar forum to me, with a thread titled *"ArtWave scandal: character matters."* ArtWave scandal? What does he plan to do? Impugn my personality, my values? For now, the link is private, meant only for me. But... he might decide to make it public.

In any case, he's posted the same photos as in the other messages here, along with some I don't even remember taking. Whether Evan publishes everything himself or is willing to share it with a tabloid blog, it doesn't change the outcome: my life, my fears, my traumas, and my intimacy have become commodities, all laid bare for anyone to see and judge. Perhaps he senses we're plotting to frame him? Or is this just another warning?

My throat tightens, my chest constricts. I'm breathless. I feel the room shrinking, suffocating, like Evan's apartment that night he hurt me to stop me from leaving. I try to calm myself; I force myself to breathe. My phone, as if out of control, keeps vibrating with notifications, but I turn it off to silence it.

Tonight, during the ArtWave event, I'll present my series on light and rebirth. I don't know if anyone will appreciate it, but at this point, I don't care. I'll do my best; I'll give everything I have, everything I am.

I lie back on the bed and close my eyes. I think only of how soon I'll see Luke again. Of the trust I now feel in him. Of this new feeling that is setting my heart and senses ablaze, like a living flame. And, at this point, I just want to live and let myself burn. Unleashing, inside and outside of me, all the light

I'm capable of, in the most intense and fierce image I've ever held. That of myself and of the man who could become my destiny. The love I've always sought and who, perhaps when I least expected it, has finally found me.

CHAPTER 12

Luke

Everything is ready for the big event. Perhaps I'm not entirely prepared. However, I have no intention of withdrawing. Never again, starting from now.

The High Tide observation deck has been set up for the occasion, under the supervision of Sarah and Mars, with projectors directed at the cliffs, coloured lasers darting around to create evocative light displays, and audio consoles on stands marking out the surrounding space to prevent sound from escaping. Around me, the guests are dressed in evening gowns and, at this very moment, waiting for what has been called the "white space," a completely unplanned event that is drawing the attention and curiosity of many. Sarah has scheduled a twenty-minute event, referring to it as an "experiential interlude." Only Mars, Arden, and I know it will be a genuine battleground.

I stand at the end of the glass walkway, waiting. I look flawless and in top form, dressed in my midnight blue suit and white shirt. But inside, I'm so excited I can hardly keep my composure.

Suddenly, lurking on the right side, I spot Evan. Elegant and refined as ever, a drink in his hand, sipping with satisfaction, a smile of someone already expecting victory, a resounding success. Clearly, he's waiting for his turn, which we were forced to schedule immediately after the main screening. He fixes his triumphant gaze on me. He still doesn't know what's in store for him, the bastard. I want to smile too, but I hold back so as not to arouse his suspicions.

My mother is sitting in the front row, in the centre seat. After escorting Arden to her room, I asked to meet her, and she agreed to meet me at my apartment before we get ready for the evening. From the look she gave me as soon as she entered, she seemed already aware, or perhaps resigned, about what the topic of our conversation would be.

In any case, she allowed me to speak and express myself without interrupting or contradicting me. I told her about my relationship with Keith during college and her reaction to it. Then I told her about my meeting with Arden and what it did to me from the first time I saw him, from the first moment our eyes met on the beach. She listened to me in silence, her lips pressed together, her gaze absorbed, neither stopping nor condemning me.

'This is who I am, Mom. I'm sorry that who I am doesn't meet your expectations of me, but as much as I'd like to please you and gain your approval, I can't do anything to change that. Not when it comes to my heart, my feelings.'

'I understand, Luke.' Those were the first words she said to me at the end of my account. 'Besides, I had already understood it years ago, even if I couldn't accept it. I hoped it was just a phase, but... the other day, seeing you with Arden, I realised that's not the case.'

Now I notice her tightening her large cream-coloured shawl around her shoulders. Although she's unaware of the unpleasant situation with Evan or our plan, she seems a bit tense; I'm unsure whether she's feeling cold or anxious.

Shifting my gaze, I see Mars emerge from one side of the stage. Meanwhile, the lights fade, and Sarah appears behind me.

'Let's get this ball rolling, boss,' she whispers in my ear, a glint of malice in her amused gaze. 'We've assembled an army of fighters, even if they're staying well-hidden for now. We're going to give that slimy worm a proper surprise!'

I nod with conviction. However, I can't help but tremble inside when I think of Arden. Even if he agreed with our plan, perhaps we shouldn't expose him in this way. Unfortunately, there was nothing else we could do to stop Evan and, at the same time, publicly reveal his misdeeds. Moreover, we were forced to act under extremely tight deadlines.

Mars moves towards the centre and raises a fan he's holding in his hands. The first stolen image flashes on the giant LED screen: Arden and I laughing in the water, on the first day we surfed together, and I tried to teach him to balance on the board. Along with the image, a tag appears that reads *"New trophy?"*

As expected, a murmur, growing louder and more intense, rises from the audience, accompanied by flashes of several mobile phones. But before the overall shock is fully absorbed, the image dissolves and then reappears with a bright red overlay of the word REBIRTH, written in large letters.

Mars, meanwhile, recites some verses:

'*What you call a trophy is a castaway who has learned to swim through a thousand storms. And he hasn't given up yet.*'

Before the audience can react, the second image appears. It's Arden, a picture of him naked (but in this case partially covered for technical reasons) from a few years ago, with a piercing light from outside illuminating his body and his distressed expression. Mars opens his fan but immediately snaps it shut. The figure is reflected in four digital mirrors, rotates, and finally explodes. The word SURVIVE appears above, in white letters.

The audience holds its breath. And so do I, actually. Then some begin to applaud instinctively, though a little disoriented. Meanwhile, I notice that Evan, still standing in the same place, seems disconcerted. But he remains still.

A third sequence of images shows Arden with me again, our laughter on the surfboard, in the waves, and even on the beach. Photographs captured by Mars and Sarah, during our time together. This time, the overlay is a crescendo of words and light, chosen by Arden along with the guys: COURAGE, LIFE, FREEDOM.

Meanwhile, Mars recites some verses that feel like knives and caresses at the same time. And it is precisely at that moment that, completely unexpectedly, at least for the audience and especially for Evan Clarke, the others appear. Arden's images are then overlaid by those of the ones Evan has blackmailed and ruined over the years. With a full account and stories of his deeds, threats, and manipulations.

The spotlights finally converge on him, on Evan. A circle of light isolates him, emphasising, in a way, his misdeeds. The audience begins to understand and, immediately after, judge. They express their disapproval through an indignant murmur and even a few whistles. Evan looks around, as if searching for a non-existent ally, then steps back, casting a hateful glance at me and then at Arden, who has just appeared beside Mars and the others. Finally, he disappears, pushing his way through the guests and shoving them aside as if they were obstacles in his path.

The presentation of the facts concludes, and the scene halts. The screen turns black and seems to fade away. Instead, it takes shape, and the words LIGHT IN THE CRACKS appear in liquid gold. Then, immediately afterwards, in a luminous blue hue, LIGHT AMONG THE WAVES. Arden's main works follow, along with all the others.

The audience remains silent, seeming absorbed or perhaps still stunned by what has just taken place.

Then, however, I hear the sound of applause, gentle and barely audible. It's Jocelyn, my mother. Others join her, and the applause grows louder and more thunderous.

I look at my mother and see her with her hands on her chest, as if holding back the emotion that has overcome her, and her eyes shining. I glance at Arden and then decide to approach her, even though I'm still hesitant. But my mother doesn't wait; she gets up and comes towards me, taking my face in her hands.

'What you've created, Luke... it's wonderful, truly wonderful.' I sense her trembling, trying to hold back her emotions. 'And I'm proud of you, of what I've seen.'

'Thank you, Mom,' I smile and stroke her back. 'But the truth is, it was Arden and the guys who brought this magnificent work to fruition. I did very little.'

'You defended and protected the person you love.' She tilts her face, tears shining in her eyes. 'I think it's a lot, though.'

At her words, it's as if a wall inside me crumbles. I nod and bite my lip, trying not to break down. I know it's not the right moment yet. I must hold on, at least a little longer.

'Now go,' my mother encourages me, nodding to Arden. 'Go to him.'

I nod and set off with a determined stride, just as the main lights come back on and Sarah announces Arden's latest reworked work: "BACKLIGHT".

A single image appears on the screen, but it consists of two backlit silhouettes barely touching in front of the Pacific. I can easily recognise us; it's us. The sky is tinged with gold, and the waves are such an intense blue they look painted.

Arden, his white shirt rolled up to his elbows, quickly runs a hand through his dishevelled brown hair. His face looks tired but shows excitement at the same time.

I don't stop; I walk deliberately towards him and stand beside him by the screen.

'You are light, pure light.' These are the first words I say to him, and in truth, they are the ones I feel inside.

'Only because of you. You taught me to shine.'

There's no longer a stage, not even an audience, not for us. It's just us, two points crossing paths. I grasp him by the nape and kiss him, without restraining my impulse, without concealing my heart.

Meanwhile, behind us, the image captured by Arden nearly seems to overlap with us, demanding our attention once again, centre stage. And the audience erupts into a standing ovation, amidst festive applause and shouts of genuine joy.

Arden and I embrace, while Sarah cheers with almost exaggerated enthusiasm. Mars leaps joyfully, and all the other collaborators and attendees also appear pleased with the evening's success. I turn to look for my mother, noticing her smile and nod as she wipes away a tear.

I gently caress Arden's side, then reach for his hand, holding it in mine.

'We did it, Luke.'

'Yes, definitely.'

It's true. We did it. We reprogrammed our world and changed a destiny that would have kept us apart, distant.

We exchange a knowing glance. Everything begins now for us, from this moment, from discovering ourselves, our story. And, as far as I'm concerned, I truly want to live this story, savour it. Without fear, without hiding. Loving and allowing myself to be loved.

EPILOGUE

One year later

Arden

The ocean roars in my ears, but I am no longer afraid of its waves. Not even the tallest and broadest ones. Luke is close to me, his shadow on my board sliding parallel to mine. The headwind, instead of disturbing and hindering me, opens my lungs and boosts my confidence.

Currently, it's pressing against me, yet my board is speeding up. I can finally truly feel the light, even through the cracks. More than I would have dared hope. My light among the waves.

'I've become a champion, see?' I glance at Luke, raising my arms and maintaining perfect balance.

'Sure, champion! But don't get distracted, or you could face a nasty end and swallow a good chunk of the Pacific!' He teases me, as always.

'I'm not even thinking about it, honey!' I burst out laughing and wink at him. 'This is the classic example of the student surpassing the master!'

I turn, almost abruptly, to face a new wave. But the damn thing catches me off guard, I lose my balance and fall into the water.

'There, what did I tell you?' Luke laughs heartily, jumps off his board and joins me.

'I did it on purpose, I swear!' I raise my arms, then reach out and grab him, pulling him closer.

'Sure, absolutely!'

Luke wraps his arms around me and steals a kiss. I release my hold and smile. Then we grab our boards, climb back up, and glide smoothly towards the shore.

Meanwhile, the early morning sun softly streaks across the water, casting glimmers of light. A thought crosses my mind.

This life is mine, and I want to live it with all my heart, embracing all the joy and love I can. Because this time, my dream will not be shattered. This time, I have everything I need to be truly happy, to feel part of a world that belongs to me, just as I belong to it, as I have from the very first moment.

Luke

When the board vibrates beneath my feet, I feel the water pulling me towards an explosion of pure adrenaline. And that's exactly how I feel with Arden, most of the time. Over the course of a year, my feelings towards him haven't changed. In fact, they've grown. It's as if our bodies and our breaths have merged into one. I've never felt anything like this about anyone else.

It's always like this between us. Even when we joke and tease each other.

Arden has told me several times that I saved him, but the truth is different. He saved me. While I may have helped defend him and release him from Evan's destructive madness, he did more. He rescued me from myself, from the one who risked becoming my worst enemy.

Once we reach the shore with our boards, I pull him back towards me. He looks at me and frowns slightly.

'Is everything okay?' He tilts his face.

'Yes, almost too well.'

I smile and gently touch his face, then follow the curve of his cheekbone with my lips. Arden releases his hold, tilting his head back briefly, then claims my mouth, kissing me passionately.

'Today marks one year...'

There, then, he was also thinking about it. A year had passed since our first meeting, right here on this very beach. I nod, narrowing my eyes at him.

'The best year of my life.' I am sincere.

A year in which many things have changed for us. Perhaps not on the outside, but within us, in our souls.

'The first of many.' Arden sighs, resting his forehead against mine.

I detach myself from him for a moment, looking into his eyes. I sometimes struggle to express my feelings for him. I can't explain how happy this man makes me, how much warmth and joy he has brought into my life. Even my relationships with my mother and my colleagues have improved significantly since he arrived.

'That day, when we met...'

'I was scared shitless, Luke. That's the truth.' He answers me before I even ask the question. 'I really wanted to run away, but...'

'I know, it was the same for me.' I sigh, touch his cheek, and nod. 'But I couldn't let you go, Arden. I simply couldn't.'

'I would have fled to the other side of the world to avoid you, to prevent falling head over heels for you. But, at the same time, something inside me screamed at me to stay, to take the risk. Because, deep down, I already knew.'

'What did you already know, my love?'

'That you're the one for me, Luke.' As our eyes lock, our lips seek each other once more. 'Because you've been the one from the very beginning.'

About the author:

Facebook: https://www.facebook.com/justicewilloughbyauthor

Instagram: https://www.instagram.com/justicewilloughbyauthor